The Joke Machine

The Joke Machine

Alexander McCall Smith

illustrations by Ian Bilbey

BLOOMSBURY

For Ian and Andrew Copping

Published in Great Britain in 2006 by Bloomsbury Publishing Plc,
36 Soho Square, London, W1D 3QY

First published by Blackie and Son Ltd, 1990

A CIP catalogue record of this book is available from the
British Library

ISBN 0 7475 8050 2
9780747580508

Printed in Great Britain by Clays Ltd, St Ives Plc

1 3 5 7 9 10 8 6 4 2

All papers used by Bloomsbury Publishing are natural, recyclable products
made from wood grown in well-managed forests.
The manufacturing processes conform to the environmental
regulations of the country of origin.

www.mccallsmithbooks.co.uk
www.bloomsbury.com

CHAPTER 1

A Very Peculiar Discovery

Jeffrey had a Saturday job in a junk shop. Other boys had newspaper rounds, and earned pocket money by stuffing newspapers through front doors. Jeffrey had tried that, but had never really enjoyed waking up early on cold mornings. And so, when the owner of the junk shop, Mr Prendergast, asked him whether he'd like to help out on Saturdays, Jeffrey did not take long to make up his mind.

It was not much of a shop really. Mr Prendergast had run it for almost forty years, and in all that time it had hardly changed. Outside, in peeling paint, there was a sign which read: PRENDERGAST'S ANTIQUES. This made people stop, but once they looked in the window they realised that it was not so much antiques that were sold there as good, old-fashioned junk.

'People may say all this is rubbish,' said Mr Prendergast, pointing to the shelves stacked with dusty old bits and pieces. 'But everything here has a use. You take that old tin box up there.'

Jeffrey looked up at the tin box on the second highest shelf.

'It just looks like an old tin box, doesn't it?' Mr Prendergast went on. 'But if you open it up, you find that it's a machine for counting coins. It was used in a bank a long time ago, and it still works perfectly.'

'And that?' asked Jeffrey, pointing at a large glass jar with a red handle sticking out of its top. 'What's that?'

'That,' said Mr Prendergast proudly, 'is a butter-making machine. You put the cream in and you turn the handle, and you get butter for your efforts. And very delicious it was too, I can tell you!'

There were many other things besides. There were old flags and old trumpets; there were boxes of tarnished coins and medals;

there were ancient typewriters; and there were gramophones which only played when you wound up the handle. If anybody ever needed something old and almost impossible to find, they knew that Prendergast's was the shop to find it in.

Mr Prendergast always closed up on Fridays. On that day he would set out by himself to buy things to sell in his shop. If ever he heard of a sale or if he knew that somebody was clearing out an attic, he would be there to see if there was something old and dusty which the owner might be willing to sell him. He never failed. On Saturday mornings, when Jeffrey came in to help, there would usually be a box or two of old things to be sorted out.

'This is very useful,' Mr Prendergast would say as he lifted some strange-looking item out of the pile. 'Somebody's bound to want that!'

Or, sometimes he would say, 'I don't know

8

why I bought that. I'm sure nobody will want it. Whatever can I have been thinking of at the time?'

Jeffrey would rub the dust off the new purchases and find a place for them on the shelves. As he did so, Mr Prendergast would enter the details of each item in his book and note down the price he had paid. In this way, he would always remember what he had to charge for something, even if it was not to be sold for years to come.

One Saturday, while they were sorting out a very large box of things which Mr Prendergast had bought from somebody's attic, they came across a very peculiar machine. It was not very big – about the size of a typewriter – but it was clearly very old. On the front it had a row of keys and at the back there were wheels which could be turned to different positions. And on the right-hand side there was a lever and a place for a roll of paper.

'This really is very strange,' said Mr Prendergast, scratching his head as he spoke. 'It's rather like an old adding machine – you know, the ones they had before they invented calculators and spoiled everything. And yet . . .'

He turned it upside down and looked at it from below.

'No,' he said. 'It's not an adding machine. In fact, I have absolutely no idea at all what it could be.'

Jeffrey gazed at the machine and shook his head.

'I can't work it out either,' he said.

Mr Prendergast laughed.

'Well, I can't really sell it to somebody if I can't say what it is,' he said. 'I suppose I'd better throw it away.'

'Don't do that,' said Jeffrey. 'I could try to make it work.'

'But you don't know what it's meant to do,' replied Mr Prendergast.

'I could try to work it out,' Jeffrey said.

Mr Prendergast shrugged. 'If you really want it,' he said, handing Jeffrey the strange machine, 'then you're welcome to it. Here you go.'

CHAPTER 2

A Slight Technical Hitch

Jeffrey was kept busy in the shop that day. There were quite a few customers and there was a lot of fetching and carrying to do. At last, when the time came to go, he picked up his new machine and carried it home. It was heavier than he had imagined, and by the time he reached home he was glad to be able to set it down on the table in his room and examine it.

It was still not clear to Jeffrey what the machine was meant to do. He had seen a number of old adding machines, and he

knew how they worked, but this one was quite different. He studied the keys on the front and pressed one or two down. They moved, but only just. The machine, it seemed, was rusty.

Jeffrey knew how to deal with this problem. Fetching a can of oil, he squirted a small amount into all the holes he could see. Then he tried the keys again. This time they moved.

Next, Jeffrey tried the lever at the side. The oil took a little time to work here, but at last he managed to get it moving. As it did so, there came a whirring and clicking noise inside, and the wheels at the back began to spin round. Then, when the lever sprang back to its original position, the machine became silent again.

'Well!' said Jeffrey to himself. 'I wonder what all that was about?'

Jeffrey was sitting and pondering over his mysterious machine when his friend, Ben, arrived. Ben looked at the machine and poked about for a while with a screwdriver, then he shook his head.

'We'll never work out what it is,' he said. 'Was there a book of instructions with it?'

'No,' said Jeffrey sadly. 'There might have been instructions once, but that would have been years and years ago.'

Ben looked at the machine again.

'This place here,' he said, 'looks as if it takes a roll of paper.'

'Yes,' said Jeffrey. 'And the paper goes into the machine just there.'

Ben was now becoming excited. 'And it comes out here. Look!'

Jeffrey looked at the machine and then he looked at Ben. They had both reached the same conclusion at the same time. If they put on a roll of paper and fed it into the machine, they would find out what it did when the paper came out the other side.

'It's obvious,' Jeffrey exclaimed. 'We should have done this right at the beginning.'

While Ben went out to buy a roll of paper from the stationery shop, Jeffrey finished cleaning the machine. Then, with the paper put into place, Jeffrey pushed the lever into the start position, took a deep breath, and pulled it down. Once again the machine made a strange whirring sound. Then there came the noise of clicking from within, rather like the sound of a typewriter working all by itself, and then there was another whirring.

'It's doing something,' Jeffrey whispered. 'It works.'

'Yes,' said Ben. 'I wonder . . .'

Before Ben could finish what he had to say, the machine gave a final whirr and a small piece of paper dropped neatly out of the other side.

Jeffrey picked up the paper and looked at it. Something had been printed on it inside the machine. He started to read, and then, to Ben's complete astonishment, he began to laugh.

'What's so funny?' Ben said. 'Let me see.'

Jeffrey handed his friend the piece of paper.

'It's a joke machine,' he said. 'That's what it is. It's printed out the funniest joke I've seen for years!'

CHAPTER 3

Mr Prendergast Has an Idea

For the next hour or so, Jeffrey and Ben experimented with the joke machine. They found that by setting the keys in different positions, the machine would come up with different jokes. Some of the keys were painted red, and if these were pushed in, the jokes would all be about funny things that happened to people at school. If a green key were pushed in, then the jokes were ones about unfortunate things happening to people, such as falling over things or into things, or having things dropped on them. And if a green key and a red key were pressed in at the same time, riddles would be printed.

'It's a wonderful machine,' Ben said. 'But do you know how it works?'

Jeffrey had no idea. He had never come across a machine capable of being funny, and he had not the slightest notion of how the joke machine functioned. All he knew was that he was now the owner of the most extraordinary machine that had ever been invented.

Neither Jeffrey nor Ben told anybody about their discovery, and it was not until the following Saturday that Jeffrey was to discuss it with anybody else.

'Do you remember that strange machine

you gave me?' he said to Mr Prendergast. 'The one that you didn't know anything about?'

'Yes,' said Mr Prendergast. 'Are you going to tell me now that you've got it working?'

'Yes,' said Jeffrey, and then, very nervously, 'You don't want it back, do you?'

'Of course not,' said Mr Prendergast. 'I gave it to you. And that means it's yours.'

'I've brought it along with me,' Jeffrey said. 'I wanted to show you how it works.'

Jeffrey showed Mr Prendergast the now shining machine.

'It certainly looks very clean,' said Mr Prendergast. 'You've made a good job of it. But what does it do?'

'You won't believe this,' Jeffrey said.

'Let's see about that,' said Mr Prendergast, with a laugh.

Jeffrey adjusted the keys of the machine and put his hand on the lever.

'Here we go,' he said. And with that he pulled the lever down and set the extraordinary whirring and clicking into motion.

Mr Prendergast adjusted his glasses on the end of his nose and peered at the machine as it shivered and shook.

'My goodness!' he said. 'It's making enough noise about it. What on earth can it be doing?'

'Just wait,' said Jeffrey.

The machine gave a final whirr and spat out the piece of paper at the other end. Jeffrey picked it up and, without reading it, gave it to Mr Prendergast.

Mr Prendergast unfolded the paper and started to read it aloud.

'Three people went up in a hot air balloon one day. One of them was very tall, and one was very short. The other was in between. The tall person said to the short person . . .' He stopped, his eyes wide with surprise as he read on to himself. Then, with a guffaw, he threw the joke up into the air.

'How hilarious!' he shouted out, tears of laughter appearing in the corners of his eyes. Then, catching the joke as it fluttered down, he handed it to Jeffrey.

'Here, Jeffrey, read this,' he said. 'See what the tall person said to the short person . . . Oh, my goodness me, how utterly and fantastically hilarious!'

'You see,' said Jeffrey. 'It's a joke machine.'

'Oh, I can see that,' said Mr Prendergast, still laughing. 'I can see that all right!'

Jeffrey printed off several more jokes for Mr Prendergast, and each time Mr Prendergast laughed more and more. Finally, after the machine had come up with a very funny riddle about a camel, they put the machine away and thought about getting on with their work.

'That's a marvellous machine you have there, Jeffrey,' said Mr Prendergast. 'What are you going to do with it?'

Jeffrey shrugged his shoulders.

'Nothing in particular,' he said. 'I thought I might just keep it at home and get it to print out one or two jokes each day.'

Mr Prendergast looked disappointed.

'But a machine like that could make you famous,' he said. 'And it could bring a lot of laughs to a lot of people. You should show it off.'

'Maybe,' said Jeffrey. 'But how could I do that?'

Mr Prendergast thought for a few moments.

'I have an idea,' he said at last. 'If you came here every Saturday, as usual, you could set the machine up in the shop. We'd put a notice in the window, telling passers-by to come in and see the machine. Who could resist a sign which said: THE WORLD'S ONLY JOKE MACHINE? And, if they wanted a joke, you could charge them a small fee to see the machine in operation.'

Mr Prendergast's idea seemed a good one to Jeffrey.

'But what about you?' he asked. 'Won't it annoy you having people coming into your shop to look at the joke machine?'

Mr Prendergast laughed.

'No shopkeeper minds people coming into his shop,' he said. 'The more people who come in to look at the machine, the more people will see other things that they want to buy. It'll suit us both.'

Jeffrey asked if it would be all right for

Ben to come in to help him show off the machine and Mr Prendergast said that he had no objection to that. Then, just before he went home that afternoon, he and Mr Prendergast made a large notice for the window of the shop.

COMING SATURDAY! the notice read. THE ONLY JOKE MACHINE IN THE WORLD. DON'T MISS IT!

CHAPTER 4
The Public Debut

The following week, Jeffrey spent more time cleaning and oiling the joke machine. He polished each key until the metal sparkled and glistened, and then he painted the handle of the lever. By the time he had finished, the joke machine looked as if it had just left the factory.

On Saturday morning he was already waiting outside the shop by the time Mr Prendergast drove up in his battered old van. Together they took the screens off the windows and turned on the lights in the shop's dim interior. Then, once Ben had arrived and the joke machine was proudly displayed on its own table, they waited for the first person to come in.

Mr Prendergast's shop was in a good position – in the middle of a row of other shops. This meant that there were always plenty of people passing along the pavement and, of course, everybody looked into his window to see what interesting old things he might be displaying. When the first shoppers arrived, Jeffrey noticed them stop and read the poster in the window.

'Look,' he said to Mr Prendergast. 'They're interested.'

'I told you they would be,' said Mr Prendergast. 'Now let's see if they come in.'

It was not long before a small crowd had

gathered outside the window. There was an excited buzz of conversation from the shoppers and then the first person pushed open the door and came in. He was followed by

others, and soon there was a knot of people standing about Jeffrey's table, peering at the extraordinary machine.

'Is there really such a thing as a joke machine?' asked a woman with a large hat. 'Or is this all a bit of a joke?'

'No,' replied Jeffrey. 'It's not a joke at all. Joke machines really do exist – and this is one.'

A boy standing beside the woman looked closely at the machine and tried to press one of the keys.

'No you don't!' Jeffrey said sharply. 'You have to know what you're doing to work this.'

'Show us then,' said a man at the back. 'Prove that this is a joke machine.'

'Yes,' echoed another. 'You can't fool us that easily!'

There were murmurs of agreement from other members of the crowd and Jeffrey looked at Mr Prendergast for support.

'Now then,' said Mr Prendergast in a brisk

voice. 'Those who want jokes can pay for them. We have our expenses to meet.'

The man who had urged Jeffrey to prove the machine stepped forward. Reaching into his pocket, he took out a coin and flipped it over to Ben.

'All right,' he said. 'But if it doesn't work, I want my money back – twice over!'

Jeffrey nodded to Ben and told people to stand back. Then, adjusting the keys, he pushed the lever. When the sound of whirring and clicking was heard, several people in the crowd drew in their breath.

'It is working,' one whispered to another.

'Yes,' said another. 'And look at all those wheels going round and round.'

After a while, the machine stopped making a noise and there, exactly as Jeffrey had expected, was the printed piece of paper. Jeffrey took the joke and handed it to the man who had paid for it.

The man unfolded the paper dubiously. Then he read the joke to himself. There was a pause. Everybody in the crowd was looking at the man's face, watching for his reaction.

'Come on,' said a boy at the back. 'Tell it to us.'

'Maybe it's not so funny,' chipped in another. 'See – he's not laughing.'

The man turned round to face the others.

'Oh my!' he said suddenly. 'What a joke!'

And with that he began to laugh.

'Share the joke!' somebody called. 'Come on!'

But the man was too busy laughing.

'I'm sorry,' he said, spluttering between his laughs. 'I just can't speak very . . . very . . . Oh my!'

He tucked the joke into his pocket, put on his hat, and went chuckling out of the shop.

'There goes a satisfied customer,' remarked Mr Prendergast. 'Now, who's next?'

CHAPTER 5

Mr Jenkinson Makes a Scene

Jeffrey and Ben sold almost one hundred jokes that Saturday. After the first customer had gone off laughing, everybody else was keen to get their own joke. Mr Prendergast lined the customers up so that each could be served in turn. Ben took the money and Jeffrey operated the machine. Nobody was dissatisfied with his or her joke. Everybody laughed, and some laughed so much that they cried. One girl found her joke so funny that she fell on the floor, holding her sides, and had to be revived with a glass of water. Another person laughed so much that he had a bad attack of hiccups and had to have a cold spoon inserted down the back of his shirt to make the hiccups stop. Mr Prendergast provided the spoon from one of his shelves, and the man liked it so much that he bought it.

At first the joke machine worked steadily and without a hitch. Then, after the twentieth joke, Jeffrey noticed that the lever was becoming rather warm to the touch.

'Is it overheating?' he asked Ben.

Ben shook his head. 'I don't see why it should,' he replied. 'And the jokes are still coming.'

So Jeffrey continued to sell jokes and ignored the steadily growing warmth of the lever. After the fiftieth joke, though, he saw what he thought was a small wisp of smoke emerging from the top of the machine, and twenty jokes later the machine began to shake.

'We'll have to stop,' Jeffrey said. 'We must let it cool down.'

This time, Ben agreed, but no sooner had he done so than the machine began to emit a highpitched whine, rather like a kettle on the boil.

'Look out!' shouted Jeffrey. 'It's going to explode!'

At this, all the customers in the shop made a dash for the door. Jeffrey sheltered behind a table and Ben dived beneath a chair. From his hiding place, Jeffrey watched the machine leap about on the table until slowly it began to calm down. After ten minutes or so, he and Ben emerged and approached the now silent machine.

'Should we try it again?' Jeffrey asked uneasily.

Ben looked doubtful at first, but after a few moments' thought he nodded his head.

Jeffrey set the controls gingerly and then pressed the lever. The machine felt much cooler now and the joke, when it came, was all about Eskimos.

'I think it's cooled down,' he said with relief. 'But we'll still have to be careful not to overwork it.'

Nothing further went wrong, and when they closed the shop that evening, Mr Prendergast was beaming with pleasure.

'I've never had so many people in the shop at one time,' he said. 'And quite a few of them bought things. I sold a cabin trunk, two telescopes, and an old hat rack. And I mustn't forget that spoon!'

Jeffrey was pleased that Mr Prendergast was so happy with the arrangement. He offered Mr Prendergast a share of his takings from the jokes, but Mr Prendergast refused. So Jeffrey divided the money between himself and Ben and together they tidied up.

'I can't wait for next Saturday,' Ben said as they walked home.

'Neither can I,' said Jeffrey. 'Word will have got round by then. I expect there'll be even more people.'

Jeffrey was right. The following Saturday, not only did some of the people who had already bought jokes come for more, but they brought their friends as well. By ten o'clock in the morning there was a line of people stretching out of the shop and down the street. Everybody in town, it seemed, wanted to see the wonderful joke machine in operation. Jeffrey and Ben were careful, though, to give the machine a rest from time to time. Joke machines could clearly be dangerous, and they did not want what happened last week to happen again.

Half-way through the day, when Jeffrey was having a break and Ben was working the machine, Mr Prendergast called him to the back of the shop.

'I'm afraid we're in trouble,' he said quietly. 'Look through the window.'

Jeffrey looked through the window at the side of the shop. There, standing in the middle of the road, his face full of fury, was the owner of the next-door shop. It was Mr Jenkinson, a notoriously bad-tempered man. He had never had more than one or two

words to say to Mr Prendergast and even these few words were hardly very friendly.

'He looks very unhappy,' Jeffrey said. 'What's wrong?'

'He's cross about the crowds,' Mr Prendergast replied. 'He hates the thought

of so many people having a good time –
right under his nose. Look! He's beginning
to shake with rage.'

Jeffrey watched Mr Jenkinson staring at
the line of happy people. It seemed as if he
was going to explode with anger.

'I shouldn't be surprised if he's called the
police,' Mr Prendergast said. 'It's just the
sort of thing he'd do.'

Mr Prendergast was right. A few minutes
later, a policeman arrived at the door of the
shop, accompanied by an angry-looking Mr
Jenkinson.

'There he is,' said Mr Jenkinson, pointing
at Mr Prendergast. 'And that boy with him,
he's in it up to his neck as well.'

The policeman looked a bit awkward.

'I'm sorry, sir,' he said to Mr Prendergast.
'Mr Jenkinson insisted that I come to see
what was happening here. He's complained
about the disturbance.'

Mr Prendergast smiled. 'Well, officer, all
that's happening here is that we're selling a

good line in jokes. And, as you can see for yourself, they're proving rather popular.'

The policeman looked at all the people. Then he looked at Mr Jenkinson.

'I don't see anything wrong with that,' he said after a while. 'I can't see any laws being broken.'

'Precisely,' agreed Mr Prendergast. 'There's no law against enjoying yourself.'

'And surely it's not a crime to be happy,' added Jeffrey.

Mr Jenkinson looked at Jeffrey and shook a fist at him.

'You keep out of it,' he snarled.

'Now, now,' said the policeman. 'I won't have any arguing, if you don't mind.'

Then he turned to Mr Jenkinson.

'I don't think you've really got any cause for complaint,' he said. 'I'm sorry.'

Mr Jenkinson cast an angry glance at Jeffrey and then an even angrier one in the direction of the joke machine.

'Ha!' he hissed. 'Joke machine indeed!

Whoever heard of such nonsense!' And with that, he stormed out, pushing rudely past the people who were waiting for their chance to see the machine.

The policeman said that he considered the matter closed, as long as the crowd behaved itself. Then, with Jeffrey and Mr Prendergast standing by, Ben printed out a joke for him. It was a good joke, all about a policeman and two robbers whose shoes didn't fit. The policeman thought it very funny and his laughter could be heard for some time as he walked back down the street.

CHAPTER 6

Out of Order

By the time he arrived at the shop the next Saturday, Jeffrey had forgotten all about the unpleasantness with Mr Jenkinson. Mr Prendergast, though, seemed worried about something.

'I'm not at all sure,' he said, 'but I have a feeling that somebody's been in here.

Nothing's missing, but, well, not everything's quite in place.'

'Has there been a burglar?' asked Jeffrey.

Mr Prendergast looked doubtful. 'I don't think so,' he said. 'But I think somebody's been in. But why, I don't know. All the locks are still on the doors and none of the windows is broken.'

'Perhaps it's your imagination,' Jeffrey said, as he took the cover off the joke machine. 'Perhaps a cat got in and knocked over a few things.'

'Perhaps,' said Mr Prendergast uncertainly.

As they had expected, by the time they had opened the shop there was a good crowd of people waiting to see the joke machine working. Some of the people had come from neighbouring towns, as the fame of the joke machine had spread. There was even a reporter from the local newspaper, and a photographer to take photographs. Jeffrey and Ben were used to all the fuss by now,

and were quite calm as they prepared the machine for its first task.

The first customer was a girl who had already seen the machine on the previous two Saturdays. She paid her money and waited for her joke, a broad smile across her face. Jeffrey pulled the lever and waited for the joke to appear. The photographer from the newspaper hovered about, his flash-gun popping as he photographed the working of the amazing machine.

Jeffrey handed the piece of paper to the girl, who opened it and read it.

'What?' she said, and then, 'Is that meant to be funny?'

Jeffrey took the piece of paper from her and read what the machine had printed. He scratched his head, trying to see if he had somehow missed the joke, and passed it on to Ben. Ben read it too and wrinkled up his nose.

'I don't think that's at all funny,' he said. 'Perhaps we didn't push the keys in properly. Shall we try again?'

This time they were very careful in their setting of the machine. They checked everything and then checked it again before the lever was pulled. Then they stood back as the machine whirred and clicked in its normal way. Then, as if everything were perfectly normal, it ejected the paper at the other end.

Jeffrey took the joke and handed it to the girl.

'I'm sure that will be all right,' he said.

The girl read the joke and shook her head.

'It's not,' she said. 'It's not in the least bit funny. Please may I have my money back!'

Jeffrey gave her her money back. Then, after quietly discussing the matter with Ben and Mr Prendergast, they agreed that they would have to suspend the sale of jokes for that day.

'I'm sorry,' he announced to the expectant crowd. 'The joke machine is out of order.'

There were rumbles of disappointment as the people drifted away. The reporter closed his notebook with a snap, shook his head doubtfully, and left with the disgruntled photographer.

'I might have known it was all nonsense,' he murmured as he left the shop. 'A joke machine just isn't possible!'

While Mr Prendergast attended to his business, Jeffrey and Ben pored over the joke machine. They tried it again at least ten times, taking great care to set the keys correctly, but each time the machine failed to print anything funny. Half the time, now, it printed nonsense, and the other half it printed out things which were either unfunny or even sad.

'There's something badly wrong with it,' Jeffrey said. 'And I have no idea how to fix it.'

'Let's open it up,' Ben suggested. 'We might be able to see what's gone wrong.'

Jeffrey was a bit reluctant to open the machine, but he realised that they really had no alternative. Ben fetched a screwdriver and together they took off the back of the machine.

Inside the machine, there was a bewildering array of parts. Alongside ratchets and brackets, there were widgets and cratchets. At the top, amidst a forest of spindles there were flanges, both sprung and unsprung. And as for sprockets – there was any number of those.

Jeffrey looked at Ben, who sighed.

'Well,' Ben said. 'How on earth can we even begin to begin?'

'We can't,' said Jeffrey sadly. 'We'd just make things even worse.'

And then he noticed the name of the factory, printed neatly on a small metal plate.

'We could write to them,' Jeffrey said. 'We could ask them to send us a book of instructions on how to do repairs.'

'Yes,' said Ben. 'I suppose we could. If . . .'

'If what?' asked Jeffrey.

'If the factory still exists,' said Ben. 'After all, this machine is terribly old.'

Jeffrey nodded. He knew that there was hardly any chance that there would still be anybody at the address, but there was no harm in trying, and he would try.

CHAPTER 7

In Need of Repair

Nothing happened that week. Every day, Jeffrey asked Mr Prendergast whether any mail had arrived for him at the shop, and each day the answer was the same. That Saturday they left a notice in the window: THE JOKE MACHINE IS STILL OUT OF ORDER. Hardly anybody came into the

51

shop now, and Mr Prendergast seemed quite miserable.

Mr Jenkinson was pleased. They saw him standing outside his shop, smirking with pleasure at the fact that the crowds of happy people had gone away.

Then, the following Wednesday, Mr Prendergast called at Jeffrey's house with an envelope. He had run all the way from his shop and was red in the face from the effort.

'It arrived this morning,' he panted. 'I decided to bring it straight round.'

Jeffrey opened the letter with fumbling hands. He hardly dared hope that it was from the factory but . . . Yes! It was!

'Read it out,' said Mr Prendergast impatiently. 'Let's hear it.'

'Your letter came as a great surprise,' Jeffrey read. 'We only made one or two of those machines and that was many years ago. For some reason, we stopped making them and went on to making vacuum cleaners. Nobody here remembers the reason why, but that's what we did.

'Anyway, we still have somebody in the factory who remembers those machines. He's very old and we keep him on to oil the cogs in the suckers in the vacuum cleaners. He's very busy, but he has agreed to come and see you next Friday at three o'clock. We

hope that he'll be able to fix your machine, although we must say that we can't promise anything.'

Mr Prendergast gave a whoop of delight.

'That's marvellous,' he said. 'With any luck we'll be back in business by Saturday.'

The repair man arrived at exactly the time the letter had promised. Jeffrey was waiting for him at the door of the shop and welcomed him as he entered. His hair was quite white and his hands were gnarled with age, but when he took the screwdriver out of his bag of tools and had the cover off the machine in a flash, Jeffrey knew that here was somebody who knew exactly what he was doing.

'Mmm,' he said, as he shone a torch into the inside of the machine. And then, after a moment or two, he added, 'Ah hah!'

'Can you see what's wrong?' Jeffrey asked anxiously. 'Can you fix it?'

'Mmm,' said the repair man again, as he

fiddled about in the machine. 'This is very peculiar.'

Jeffrey craned his neck to see. He saw the screwdriver probing and prodding, but it was difficult to make out what was happening.

At last the repair man stood up.

'Somebody's been fiddling about in there,' he said suspiciously. 'Several of the wheels have been pushed out of place and one or two screws have been taken out.'

'It wasn't me,' Jeffrey said quickly. 'I looked inside, but I didn't touch anything.'

'I see,' said the repair man. 'Well, I've fixed it. It should work perfectly well now.'

Jeffrey felt a flush of relief.

'Are you going to try it out now?' he asked.

'Yes,' said the repair man. 'But first I want to show you something very interesting. Would you like to see it?'

Jeffrey crouched down beside the repair man as they both peered into the inside of the machine.

'These are strange machines,' the old man said. 'I was the one who made them, you know. And I'm probably the only person alive who knows their very special secret.'

Jeffrey held his breath, hoping that the old man would not stop.

'There's a special setting,' the repair man went on. 'If you push the first three keys down and at the same time you twist this wheel at the back a little bit like this . . . and then a little bit like that . . . and then you do this . . . and finally do that . . . I hope you're remembering all this . . . then the machine will produce the funniest joke ever heard.' He paused. 'But there's one problem with that. The strain on the machine is so much that it can only produce one such joke in its lifetime. If you try to get it to do it more than once, it will explode. And that,' he finished off, 'will be the end of that.'

Jeffrey knew what the repair man meant. He still remembered how frightened he had been when the machine had overheated. He was quite sure that if the machine did explode, then that would be the end not only of the machine, but probably also of the shop itself.

CHAPTER 8

Back in Business

The joke machine worked perfectly. Jeffrey thanked the repair man, who brushed aside his offer to pay him for his help.

'It's been a pleasure to see one of these machines again,' he said. 'And I hope that it never lets you down again.' He paused at the door for a moment, shaking his head dubiously. 'Mind you, I still maintain that somebody interfered with it. They never go wrong by themselves, you know.'

Mr Prendergast and Jeffrey lost no time in making a new notice for the window of the shop.

BACK AT LAST! it said in large letters. THE ONE AND ONLY JOKE MACHINE! DON'T MISS IT THIS SATURDAY!

There was a air of excitement among the crowd that gathered around the notice. People rushed off to tell their friends, and those who had missed the chance to see the joke machine in the past were delighted that they would now have the opportunity. The newspaper telephoned Mr Prendergast and asked him whether it was really true and whether the joke machine could be expected to work this time. He replied that there was now absolutely no doubt as he himself had run off a joke from the machine only five minutes before.

When Saturday morning came, there was

a bigger crowd than ever before. Jeffrey and Ben had to elbow their way to the front in order to get in the door, and once they were in, the people began to call out for them to open up.

'Don't keep us waiting,' they called. 'Let's have the first joke.'

Everybody was in a very good mood – everybody, that is, except Mr Jenkinson. He peered out of the door of his shop, enraged by all the laughter and good-natured calls from the crowd.

'Curse them!' he muttered under his breath. 'How dare they stand about laughing and joking! I don't see what there is to laugh about!'

He was also cross, of course, that there was nobody visiting his own shop. Everybody was far too interested in what was happening in Mr Prendergast's shop to go near Mr Jenkinson's bad-tempered establishment.

When all was ready, Mr Prendergast opened the doors and let people in. Jeffrey and Ben stood behind the table, Ben taking the money and giving tickets for a joke while Jeffrey operated the machine. Mr Prendergast stood behind his counter, beaming in happiness at the sight of the joyful crowd.

The machine was in fine order. Since the repair man had tinkered with it, the jokes it was printing out seemed funnier than ever, and people were delighted with what they got. Some asked for more than one joke and laughed twice as long over the second and three times as hard over the third.

Finally, at the end of the afternoon, the time came to serve the last customer.

'I'm sorry,' Mr Prendergast called out to those who were still waiting. 'It's time to close. But the joke machine will be in operation next Saturday, as usual, and you can get your jokes then.'

The last of the people went off, disappointed at not getting their jokes, but looking forward to next Saturday. Mr Prendergast shut the door and sighed with relief.

'That's the busiest day I've ever had,' he said to Jeffrey. 'I've sold so much that I've lost track of it all.'

He sat down on a chair and mopped his brow.

'Why don't you go home right now,' Jeffrey said. 'Ben and I can sweep the floor and close up the shop for you.'

Mr Prendergast looked up thankfully.

'That's very kind of you,' he said. 'There's nothing I'd like more than a good long bath and a cup of tea.'

Alone in the shop, Jeffrey and Ben set to the task of clearing up. The hoards of people who had been in the shop had left a bit of a mess. Some had dropped their joke papers on the ground and left them there; others had bumped into things and not put them back in their proper place. There was a lot of work to do.

By the time that Jeffrey and Ben had finished, they were both exhausted. It was now dark outside and the shop was only dimly lit by two small bulbs that dangled from the ceiling. The two boys sat down to rest, looking about them at all the extraordinary things that lurked in the shadows of Mr Prendergast's shop.

It was then that Ben heard a noise.

'What was that?' he whispered to Jeffrey. 'I'm sure I heard something.'

Jeffrey strained his ears. He could hear the ticking of several old clocks, but that was all.

'I can't hear anything unusual,' he said. But no sooner had he spoken when there came a sound. It was a creaking sound, rather like the sound made by a loose floorboard when somebody treads on it.

'There!' whispered Ben. 'That was it.'

Jeffrey rose to his feet and peered into the dark corners of the shop. It was hard to make anything out – there were so many strange shapes. A suit of armour could be a man; a stuffed wild cat could be a leopard; everything looked threatening in the darkness.

Jeffrey heard his own breathing and felt the thumping of his heart.

'Is there anybody there?' he called out, trying to make his voice sound as strong as possible.

There was no reply.

'We heard you,' Ben called out bravely. 'We know you're there.'

They listened to the silence, glancing nervously at one another. Then, with a sudden lurch, a figure came out of the darkness. Jeffrey gasped in fright and Ben stood quite frozen with fear.

'Hallo, boys,' a voice said. 'Yes, it's me.'

CHAPTER 9

The Funniest Joke Ever Heard

There on the other side of the shop stood Mr Jenkinson.

'Don't move, boys, and you'll be quite safe,' he said. 'I've just come to deal with that irritating machine of yours.'

As he spoke, Mr Jenkinson started to move towards the table on which the joke machine stood. When he saw this, Jeffrey felt a surge of anger within him.

'No!' he shouted out, dashing towards the table. 'You leave that alone.'

Ben now acted. Snatching an old walking stick which Mr Prendergast had been trying to sell for years, he sprinted across the room to stand at his friend's side.

'Now, now,' hissed Mr Jenkinson. 'Let's not have any trouble. You can see that I'm much bigger and stronger than both of you.'

Ben waved the stick in front of him.

'But I've got the stick,' he shouted out.

Mr Jenkinson laughed.

'You ridiculous boy,' he said. 'That won't stop me.'

Slowly, he moved towards the boys, rolling up his sleeves as he did so. Jeffrey felt his knees shaking with fear, and Ben, although he was holding the stick, felt his muscles seize up in fright.

'It's no good,' Ben whispered to Jeffrey. 'He's much bigger than us.'

Jeffrey gritted his teeth. He did not want to fight, but the thought of his precious joke machine being destroyed by this wicked man was more than he could bear. Then, in a sudden flash, the memory of the repair man's words came back to him. Yes! That was it! It would be his only hope!

Mr Jenkinson now stood only a few paces away.

'Now, boys,' he said, a nasty scowl on his face. 'I'm going to give you one last chance. I shall count to ten, and if you haven't handed over that machine by then, I shall get it from you. And if you get hurt, it'll only be your fault!'

Jeffrey ran his fingers over the front of the machine. It was those three keys, wasn't it – yes, just like that. And then the wheel at the back . . . but which one?

'One,' intoned Mr Jenkinson, 'two . . .'

Jeffrey twiddled the wheel, just as the repair man had shown him. A little way that way, and then . . .

'Three,' came the icy voice of Mr Jenkinson, 'four . . .'

And a little bit that way. Then, a flick there, and a push here . . .

'Five,' went on Mr Jenkinson, 'six . . .'

And that was it. Now the lever. All the way back, and down . . .

There was the familiar sound of whirring, but this time it was louder. Then there came an unfamiliar clackety sound.

'Seven,' said Mr Jenkinson. Then, 'What's that noise? What's going on?'

Jeffrey did not reply. He now felt the machine shaking beneath him.

'Turn that thing off!' Mr Jenkinson shouted.

But the machine just continued to make a louder and louder noise. Now there were slight whiffs of smoke appearing from the top of it as the cogs and the wheels span faster and faster within it.

'It's going to explode,' said Ben. 'It's doing just what it did when it overheated.'

'No it isn't,' Jeffrey said, hoping that he had remembered the repair man's instructions correctly.

'I've wasted enough time,' said Mr Jenkinson. 'This is your last chance.'

As Mr Jenkinson spoke, the noise coming from the machine seemed to get louder and louder. It was now making the boiling kettle sound and sparks were flying out of the top.

'Duck!' shouted Ben. 'Quick! Get under the table.'

Ben and Jeffrey both flung themselves under the table, but Mr Jenkinson, who did not know what danger he was in, just stood where he was, looking in puzzlement at the over-excited machine.

Jeffrey closed his eyes and stuck his fingers into his ears. What would it be like to be in the middle of an explosion? Would you feel the bang before you heard it, or would you hear it before the shock wave hit you?

There was no explosion. Instead of a bang, Jeffrey heard Ben's voice.

'Look!' shouted Ben as he crawled out from under the table. 'It's printing a joke!'

Jeffrey opened his eyes to see the machine give a final heave and then spit out a joke. Scrambling to his feet, he snatched the paper and opened it before the astonished eyes of Ben and Mr Jenkinson. Wasting no time, he began to read out the joke that the machine had printed.

'Don't try to resist me!' shouted Mr Jenkinson, now advancing towards the boys and ignoring Ben's waving stick.

Jeffrey raised his voice so that the unpleasant shopkeeper had no choice but to hear the joke.

'I'm not listening,' shouted Mr Jenkinson.

'Oh yes you are!' shouted Ben.

Then, with a final note of triumph in his voice, Jeffrey reached the end of the joke. For a moment all three of them stayed exactly where they were. Mr Jenkinson stood as if frozen, but after a moment a smile began to move across his face.

'Read that again,' he said. 'From the beginning.'

Jeffrey did as he was told. By the time he had finished reading, Mr Jenkinson had begun to laugh. It was an extraordinary laugh — a laugh which obviously had not

'HA-HA-HA!'

been used for many years – but it became
louder and louder, until the shop rang with
the sound.

'Oh no!' he stuttered between bouts of laughter. 'That beats them all! Oh no!'

Jeffrey and Ben were laughing too. There was no doubt in Jeffrey's mind that the joke the machine had printed was the very funniest joke in all the world. Even the dreadful Mr Jenkinson, a man with no sense of humour, had been made to laugh, and now he seemed to be making up for all the lost laughter of years and years.

The three of them sat down and laughted for at least half an hour. Then Mr Jenkinson stood up, wiped his eyes, and smiled at the boys.

'I owe you an apology,' he said. 'I'm very sorry for what I tried to do.'

'That's quite all right,' said Jeffrey. 'Let's just forget it.'

But Mr Jenkinson had not yet finished.

'You see,' he said, 'I managed to get a key for the back door. I came in one night and fiddled about with your machine, just to ruin things for you.'

'I see,' said Jeffrey.

'And then, when that didn't work,' Mr Jenkinson continued. 'I decided to come and steal the machine. And I almost succeeded. But now . . .' he paused, reaching out to pat the joke machine. 'Now I realise what a terrible person I had become. I never laughed. I never smiled. I never found anything at all funny.'

'But you do now,' said Jeffrey.

'Yes,' agreed Mr Jenkinson. 'Thanks to your joke machine, I can laugh again.'

Mr Prendergast found it all very difficult to believe when Jeffrey told him what had happened in the shop that evening. On Monday, though, he realised that it was all true when he saw a beaming Mr Jenkinson standing outside his shop. When Mr Jenkinson waved to him and when he later came across to give him his apology in person, Mr Prendergast knew that the joke machine had indeed worked a miracle.

And it continued. On Saturday, when the joke machine was churning out jokes to the happy customers, Mr Jenkinson was still in a good mood. People passing by noticed it, and went into his shop to chat with him and buy a few things. This made him smile even more.

That evening, just as they were closing the shop, there was a knock on the door. There stood a smiling Mr Jenkinson.

'I've had such a good day,' he said to Jeffrey. 'I wonder if I could just have one more joke.'

'It won't be as good as your last one,' Jeffrey said. 'That was a very special one.'

'That doesn't matter,' said Mr Jenkinson. 'Now that I've found my sense of humour I can laugh at anything.'

Jeffrey agreed to run off one more joke and to give it to Mr Jenkinson, who took it and laughed long and loud.

'Well, well,' said Mr Prendergast as they watched Mr Jenkinson leave the shop. 'That's something I never thought I'd see. And it's all thanks to you.'

'No,' said Jeffrey. 'It's thanks to the joke machine.'

Mr Prendergast looked thoughtful.

'By the way,' he said. 'You never told me how that special joke went – the one which changed Mr Jenkinson. You haven't forgotten it, have you?'

Jeffrey smiled. 'It would be impossible to forget a joke like that,' he said.

So Jeffrey told the joke. And when Mr Prendergast had finished laughing – which was quite some time later – he had to agree that it was the funniest joke he had ever heard in his life.

'Oh, Jeffrey!' he said, wiping his eyes. 'Please will you do me a favour?'

'Of course,' said Jeffrey. 'What is it?'

'Tell me that joke again,' begged Mr Prendergast.

And Jeffrey did.